HELEN HANCOCKS

PENGUIN IN PERIL

templar publishing

One afternoon, three hungry cats ran out of food.

They searched the house high and low
and found three gold coins.

Dosis enormes de afecto
para mejorar su aspecto.
Besos, caricias, cosquillas...
Ni jarabes ni pastillas.
Cucamonas y achuchones.
Ni pomadas ni inyecciones.

They set off for the grocer's store.

On their way, the cats passed a cinema.

It was playing a film called *The Fishy Feast*.
They handed over the three gold coins and went in.

Later that evening,
the cats emerged from the film.

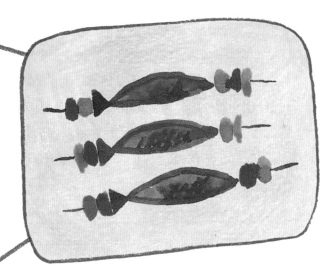

They had food on their minds
more than ever…

but the film had given them
a brilliant idea.

Around the kitchen table, they formed a cunning plan.
It would be the most brilliant robbery of all time.

Soon they would have their own fishy feast!

All they needed was…

a penguin.

One dark night, they put their cunning plan into action.

They entered the zoo
with an empty sack…

and left with a penguin.

Back home, the cats tried to tell the penguin
the next step in their plan.

They didn't speak Penguin very well…

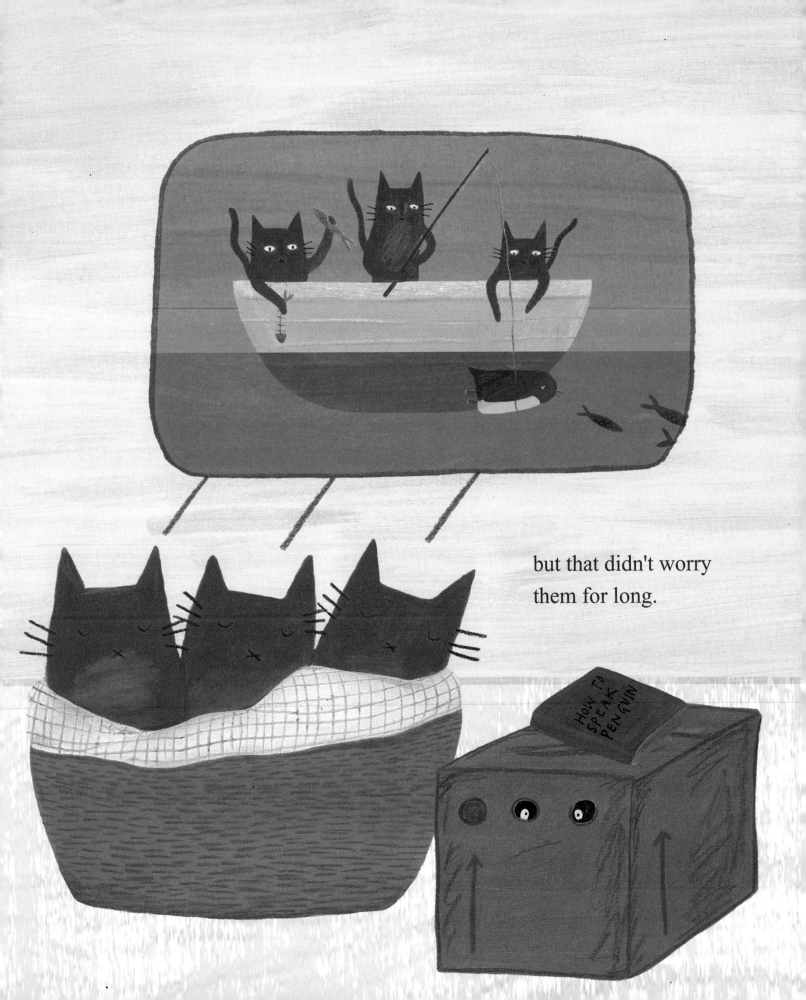

but that didn't worry
them for long.

The next day, they set off on the fishing trip.

The penguin began
to sense his perilous fate.

Anxious to get home, he
made a break for freedom.

The cats ran after him…

but the penguin proved quite difficult to spot.

They almost caught him
on the underground…

They almost caught him in a restaurant…

But the penguin was always one step ahead.

A little bird spotted the penguin
in peril. The penguin told her
that he wanted to go home.

Luckily, she knew a secret way
to the zoo.

While the cats chased
after the penguin…

the little bird had a word
with a friendly policeman.

The penguin made his escape…

PARK

ZOO

He was home!

Just in time for a fishy feast!

And as for the cats…

For my mum xx. And thank you to K and L, R, F, E, I, J, T and D for putting up with me. H. H.

A TEMPLAR BOOK

First published in the UK in 2013 by Templar Publishing, an imprint of The Templar Company Limited,
Deepdene Lodge, Deepdene Avenue, Dorking, Surrey, RH5 4AT, UK
www.templarco.co.uk

ISBN 978-1-84877-837-5 (hardback)
ISBN 978-1-84877-862-7 (softback)

Edited by Jenny Broom

Printed in China

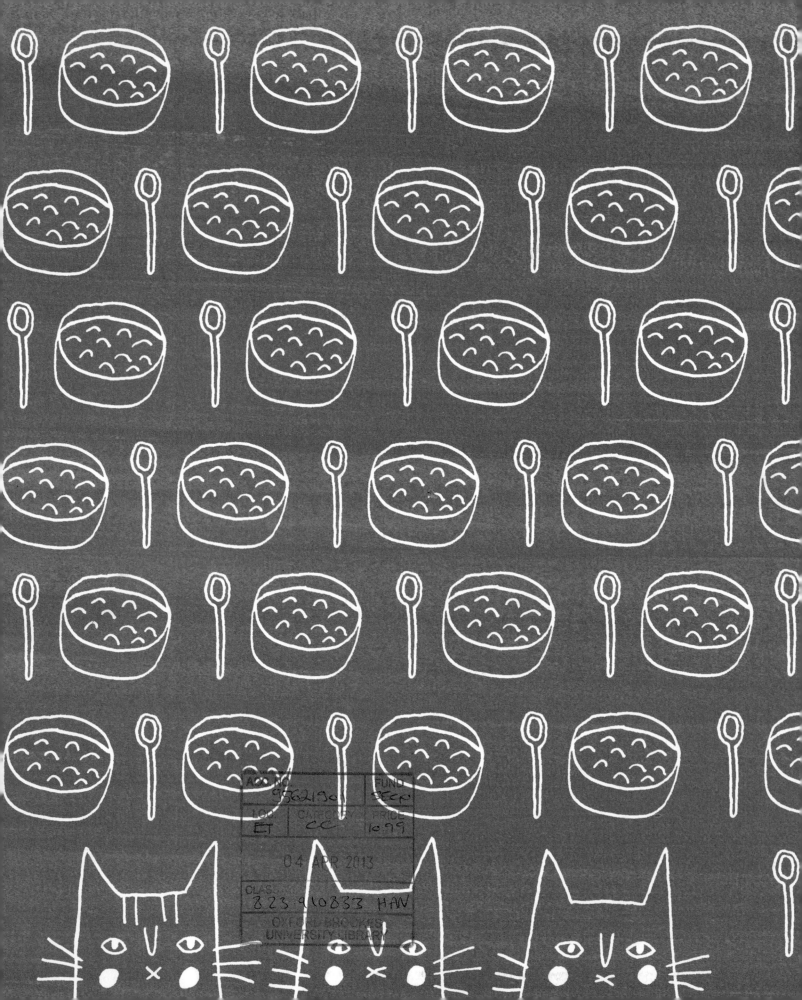